Itsy Bitsy Spider

and

Itsy Bitsy Beetle

Retold by Wes Magee
Illustrated by Tomislav Zlatic

Crabtree Publishing Company

www.crabtreebooks.com

Crabtree Publishing Company
www.crabtreebooks.com
1-800-387-7650

PMB 59051, 350 Fifth Ave.
59th Floor,
New York, NY 10118

616 Welland Ave.
St. Catharines, ON
L2M 5V6

Published by Crabtree Publishing in 2012
Printed in the U.S.A./052012/FA20120413

Series editor: Jackie Hamley
Editor: Kathy Middleton
Proofreader: Reagan Miller
Series advisor: Dr. Hilary Minns
Series designer: Peter Scoulding
Production coordinator and
   Prepress technician: Margaret Amy Salter
Print coordinator: Katherine Berti

Text (Incy Wincy Beetle/Itsy Bitsy Beetle)
© Wes Magee 2008
Illustration © Tomislav Zlatic 2008

First published in 2008
by Franklin Watts
(A division of Hachette
Children's Books)

Library and Archives Canada
Cataloguing in Publication

Magee, Wes, 1939-
      Itsy bitsy spider, and Itsy bitsy beetle / retold
by Wes Magee ; illustrated by Tomislav Zlatic.

(Tadpoles: nursery rhymes)
Issued also in electronic format.
ISBN 978-0-7787-7886-8 (bound).--ISBN 978-0-7787-
7898-1 (pbk.)

      1. Nursery rhymes, English. I. Zlatic,
Tomislav II. Title. III. Series: Tadpoles (St.
Catharines, Ont.). Nursery rhymes

PZ8.3.M34It 2012   j398.8   C2012-902473-2

Library of Congress
Cataloging-in-Publication Data

CIP available at Library of Congress

Itsy Bitsy Spider

Tomislav Zlatic

"Minibeasts are great!
They've got so many legs.
Some have 6, some 8,
and some many more!
I bet they buy lots
of shoes..."

The itsy bitsy spider climbed up the waterspout.

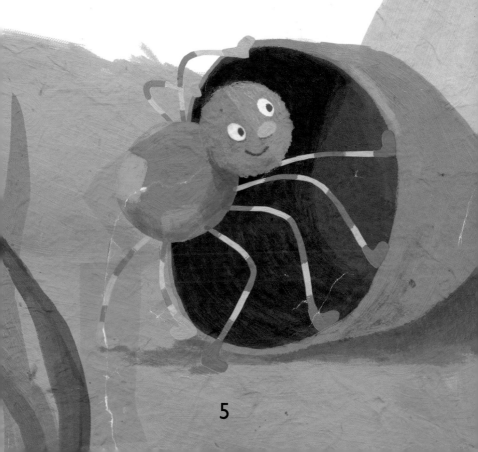

Down came
the rain

and washed
the spider out.

Out came the sun
and dried up all the rain.

9

And the itsy bitsy
spider climbed up
the spout again!

Itsy Bitsy Spider

The itsy bitsy spider
climbed up the waterspout.
Down came the rain
and washed the spider out.
Out came the sun
and dried up all the rain.
And the itsy bitsy spider
climbed up the spout again!

Can you point to the
rhyming words?

Itsy Bitsy Beetle

Wes Magee

"Lots of beetles make homes in my garden shed where it is warm and dry, and spiders climb up the plughole in the bath!"

The itsy bitsy beetle
was playing on the wall.

Down came the
snowflakes

and made the
beetle fall.

Here comes the wind
to blow the snow away

19

Now the itsy
bitsy beetle
is climbing up
to play!

Itsy Bitsy Beetle

The itsy bitsy beetle

was playing on the wall.

Down came the snowflakes

and made the beetle fall.

Here comes the wind

to blow the snow away.

Now the itsy bitsy beetle

is climbing up to play!

Can you point to the
rhyming words?

Puzzle Time!

A

B

C

D

E

What kind of weather is each picture showing?

Notes for adults

TADPOLES NURSERY RHYMES are structured for emergent readers.
The books may also be used for read-alouds or shared reading with young children.

The language of nursery rhymes is often already familiar to an emergent reader. Seeing the rhymes in print helps build phonemic awareness skills. The alternative rhymes extend and enhance the reading experience further, and encourage children to be creative with language and make up their own rhymes.

IF YOU ARE READING THIS BOOK WITH A CHILD, HERE ARE A FEW SUGGESTIONS:

1. Make reading fun! Choose a time to read when you and the child are relaxed and have time to share the story.

2. Recite the nursery rhyme together before you start reading. What might the alternative rhyme be about? Brainstorm ideas.

3. Encourage the child to reread the rhyme and to retell it using his or her own words. Invite the child to use the illustrations as a guide.

4. Help the child identify the rhyming words when the whole rhymes are repeated on pages 12 and 22. This activity builds phonological awareness and decoding skills. Encourage the child to make up alternative rhymes.

5. Give praise! Children learn best in a positive environment.

IF YOU ENJOYED THIS BOOK, WHY NOT TRY ANOTHER TITLE FROM TADPOLES: NURSERY RHYMES?

Baa, Baa, Black Sheep and Baa, Baa, Pink Sheep   978-0-7787-7883-7 RLB   978-0-7787-7895-0 PB
Hey Diddle Diddle and Hey Diddle Doodle   978-0-7787-7884-4 RLB   978-0-7787-7896-7 PB
Humpty Dumpty and Humpty Dumpty at Sea   978-0-7787-7885-1 RLB   978-0-7787-7897-4 PB

VISIT WWW.CRABTREEBOOKS.COM FOR OTHER CRABTREE BOOKS.

Answers

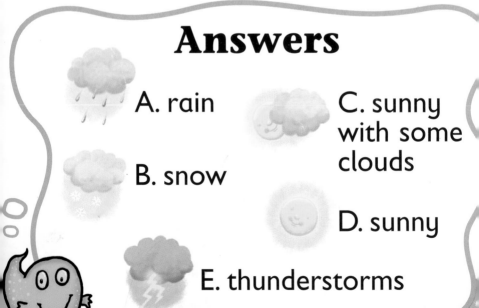

A. rain

B. snow

C. sunny with some clouds

D. sunny

E. thunderstorms